Dear Parent:
Your child's love of reading starts here!

Every child learns to read in a different way and at his or her own speed. Some go back and forth between reading levels and read favorite books again and again. Others read through each level in order. You can help your young reader improve and become more confident by encouraging his or her own interests and abilities. From books your child reads with you to the first books he or she reads alone, there are I Can Read Books for every stage of reading:

SHARED READING
Basic language, word repetition, and whimsical illustrations, ideal for sharing with your emergent reader

BEGINNING READING
Short sentences, familiar words, and simple concepts for children eager to read on their own

READING WITH HELP
Engaging stories, longer sentences, and language play for developing readers

READING ALONE
Complex plots, challenging vocabulary, and high-interest topics for the independent reader

ADVANCED READING
Short paragraphs, chapters, and exciting themes for the perfect bridge to chapter books

I Can Read Books have introduced children to the joy of reading since 1957. Featuring award-winning authors and illustrators and a fabulous cast of beloved characters, I Can Read Books set the standard for beginning readers.

A lifetime of discovery begins with the magical words "I Can Read!"

Visit www.icanread.com for information
on enriching your child's reading experience.

I Can Read Book® is a trademark of HarperCollins Publishers.

Mia and the Too Big Tutu
Copyright © 2010 by HarperCollins Publishers.
All rights reserved. Manufactured in China.
No part of this book may be used or reproduced in any manner whatsoever without written permission except in the case of brief quotations embodied in critical articles and reviews. For information address HarperCollins Children's Books, a division of HarperCollins Publishers, 195 Broadway, New York, NY 10007.
www.icanread.com
Book design by Sean Boggs

Library of Congress Cataloging-in-Publication Data is available.
ISBN 978-0-06-173302-4 (trade bdg.)— ISBN 978-0-06-173301-7 (pbk.)

15 16   SCP   10 9 8 7 6 5 ❖   First Edition

I Can Read!

SHARED
My First
READING

Mia
and the
Too Big Tutu

by Robin Farley
pictures by Aleksey and Olga Ivanov

HARPER
An Imprint of HarperCollinsPublishers

Mia wishes to be
just like her big sister.

A dancer!

Mom helps Mia's wish
come true.

It is time for class.

Mia is all set to go.

She does not forget a thing.

When Mom calls, "Ready?"
Mia grabs her bag.
She is ready!

Mia skips to school
with her bag in hand.
"Bye, Mom," calls Mia.
She does not want to be late.

"Welcome, dancers,"
sings Miss Bird.
Mia grins from ear to ear.

Mia hurries to change.
She wants to be first
on the dance floor.

Mia zips up her leotard.

She slips on her shoes.

She ties a ribbon in her hair.

Mia saves the best for last.
A pretty, pink, fluffy tutu!

The tutu is too big!
Mia packed her sister's tutu!

Mia pulls it up. It falls down.

She tugs it up.

It falls!

Mia hides.

Her heart sinks.

Mia is too bashful
to see Miss Bird now.

Mia spots her friend Ruby.
"My tutu is too big.
I'll trip!" she tells Ruby.

"My legs are too long,"
says Ruby.
"I always trip!"

The friends peek at the class.
Miss Bird is dancing sweetly.
"I like Miss Bird," says Ruby.

"I'll dance," says Mia,
"if you dance, too!"

Mia and Ruby tiptoe
onto the floor.

Mia's tutu slips. Ruby trips.

Miss Bird teaches a dance.

She spins. She leaps.

She walks on her toes!

"Who will try the dance?"
sings Miss Bird.
Nobody will try.

Miss Bird spots Mia and Ruby.
They are hiding in the back.
"Dance!" sings Miss Bird.

Mia and Ruby
are very brave.

They spin.

They leap.

They walk on their toes!

The class claps!
They cheer, too.

Mia forgets her
tutu is too big!
Mia and Ruby take a bow.

Dictionary

Leotard

(you say it like this: lee-o-tard)

The outfit that dancers wear

Pirouette

(you say it like this: pira-wet)

A very fast twirl

Tutu

(you say it like this: too-too)

A skirt that some dancers

wear over their leotards